'Tucket Teddy's Day At Work

by **Vonda** and **Bradley Cunningham**

illustrated by **Tanya Fletcher**

First Edition

Library of Congress Catalog Card Number 96-92548

ISBN 0-9653674-0-1

10 9 8 7 6 5 4 3 2 1

'Tucket Teddy™ is a trademark of Nantucket Cobblestones Limited.

Published by:

Nantucket Cobblestones Limited
One Saint Matthew's Drive
Barrington, New Hampshire 03825
(603) 942-9274

For our son, Matthew

Love,

Mom and Dad

The authors would like to thank David Rynerson, Melissa Provost, John "Newberry" Halka, Otto Appelt, Wayne "Buddy" Giorgio and Becki O'Connor for their support and suggestions. We would also like to extend special thanks to Dad Cunningham for pushing us to get this project done!

Each day of the week, from the first of May until the last of September, Chef Teddy wakes up very early in the morning to prepare for the day ahead at the Madbury Krisp Tavern.

Sometimes 'Tucket Teddy wakes up just in time to see his Dad leave for work. 'Tucket Teddy wishes that he could go along with his father to see what he does at the restaurant.

"I know that Dad cooks and bakes and tastes everything he makes . . . but what other fun things does he do during his day at work?" wonders 'Tucket Teddy out loud. "Maybe I can go to work with Dad some day soon?"

Later that week 'Tucket Teddy asks if he can spend a day at the Madbury Krisp Tavern.

"Well son, we'll be very busy all day long . . . but I'd love to have you come along!" answers Chef Teddy.

'Tucket Teddy is so excited he can hardly sleep the night before his first day at work in the restaurant.

Very early the next morning 'Tucket Teddy and his father make their breakfast and get ready for the day ahead. The sun is beginning to rise as they leave the house.

"We have a very important stop to make before getting to the restaurant, son," said Chef Teddy. "We must be the first in line to select the freshest seafood and produce!"

'Tucket Teddy is amazed at all of the fresh seafood, fruits and vegetables. He is especially interested in the live lobsters and how the fish, clams and scallops are packed in ice.

Father chooses only the best of the bunch and makes arrangements to have the seafood and produce delivered to the restaurant later in the day. The workers begin to gather Chef Teddy's order.

The tiny island of Nantucket is nearly awake. As the two Teddy's pull into the restaurant's parking lot, the smell of fresh bread fills the air. Paddy, the baker, is hard at work in the restaurant's bake shop.

Paddy has a big belly and the loudest laugh on the island. 'Tucket Teddy loves to visit the bake shop. Paddy always has a special treat for 'Tucket Teddy. Today it is a hot, gooey chocolate chip cookie.

"Work is fun!" exclaims 'Tucket Teddy.

A loud door bell announces the arrival of the day's first delivery. It is the fruits and vegetables. 'Tucket Teddy is put in charge of washing the strawberries and potatoes.

Chef Teddy is ready to start a batch of his famous clam chowder. "You've eaten in our restaurant many times son; now you know where the food comes from and how it's prepared."

The waiters and waitresses are busy making the dining room look beautiful. The wine steward rushes around preparing for the busy day ahead and one of the chefs finishes setting up the bountiful salad bar.

The telephone begins to ring and a line of customers walk into the restaurant. Many stare at Paddy's sweet creations on display in the glass case. Others wait in line to get a table in the dining room.

Chef Teddy lifts 'Tucket Teddy onto a stool in the kitchen. He adjusts his tall, white hat and the crew follows his lead. Salads are tossed and plates are washed.

As the day goes on, 'Tucket Teddy becomes very tired.

Chef Teddy announces, "One hour until dinner service," and the crew scurries about.

'Tucket Teddy's mother appears at the side door.

'Tucket Teddy can't remember the last time he has had this much fun. He got to help at the family's restaurant and now he will eat dinner with mother and father at their special table. What a wonderful day!

'Tucket Teddy dreams about strawberries, potatoes and Paddy's laugh. He tasted everything that came his way and dreamed that he would be a chef some day! 'Tucket Teddy can't wait for his next day at work in the Madbury Krisp Tavern.

Who is Madbury Krisp?

Madbury Krisp is an old man that lives in the woods of New England. He watches over the leaves on the trees and makes sure that they know when to change color for foliage season. He also puts a chill in the air that causes New Englanders to crave warm apple cider and the approaching winter months. Try this recipe after picking apples in the fall and <u>always</u> let the kids help out in the kitchen!

The Apples:

3 pounds of Macintosh apples
1 tablespoon of cinnamon
2 tablespoons of honey
1/2 cup of granulated sugar
2 tablespoons of fresh lemon juice
1/2 teaspoon of vanilla

The Krisp:

1 cup of margarine
1 1/2 cups of all purpose flour
1 cup of sugar
1 cup of quick oats
2 teaspoons of cinnamon
1 cup of chopped walnuts

1. Peel and core all apples. Cut the apples into 1/2-inch chunks and place into a medium sized mixing bowl.

2. Place all other items from the first set of ingredients into the bowl with the apples. Toss together with a wooden spoon and set aside.

3. Place all ingredients from the "Krisp" section into a large mixing bowl. Slowly rub these ingredients together with your hands (this is a good job for the kids!) until they appear crumbly.

4. Pre-heat oven to 350 degrees. Spoon the apple mixture into a 13x9x2 pan. Crumble the "krisp" mixture on top of the apples. Make sure that it is distributed evenly over the apples.

5. Place into the oven and bake for 45 minutes. The top will brown nicely when the dessert is done. Serve the Madbury Krisp in a bowl with scoops of vanilla ice cream.